SPK♥

SAVE THE SMALL MART

By Sydney Malone

ISBN 978-1-338-21025-5

10 9 8 7 6 5 4 3 2 1   18 19 20 21 22

Printed in the U.S.A.   40

First printing 2018

Book design by Erin McMahon and Carolyn Bull

SCHOLASTIC INC.

The Shopkins are watching their favorite show, *The Spatula,* together at the Small Mart.

"I'm getting tired," says Toasty Pop. "How long have we been watching this?"

Apple Blossom looks at her watch. "We've only been watching for . . . THREE WEEKS?!"

The Shopkins missed a lot of important things while they were watching TV.

Lippy Lips missed work at the Fashion Boutique. Cheeky Chocolate missed her flight for a vacation with Spilt Milk.

"I think I forgot to go to the dentist," says Toasty.

"We have to get off this couch!" says Apple Blossom.
But Apple has been there for so long that now she's stuck.
"Can someone give me a push?" she asks.

Apple checks her mail when she gets home. She got a postcard from Spilt Milk and the Small Mart power bill.

The bill is very expensive because the Shopkins watched so much TV. And they have to pay it right away!

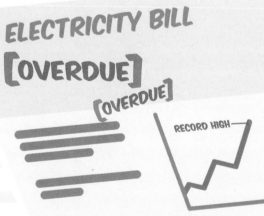

ELECTRICITY BILL
[OVERDUE]
[OVERDUE]

RECORD HIGH

[OVERDUE]

TOTAL ___ $ $ $ $ $ ___

Apple calls the Shopville mayor's office.
"We need Kooky Cookie's help," Apple Blossom tells Chip,
one of Mayor Kooky's assistants. "The Small Mart is in trouble!"

Kooky Cookie, Chip, and Chunk meet
Apple Blossom at the Small Mart.
"What happened?" Kooky asks.

"We have a huge power bill because we watched so many episodes of *The Spatula*," explains Apple Blossom. "If we don't pay the bill soon, the power will be shut off at the Small Mart!"

Kooky asks Chip and Chunk to look at the budget. They tell her there is no money left.

How will the Shopkins pay before the power is turned off?

"Let's come up with a plan to raise money for the bill and keep the Small Mart open!" declares Apple Blossom.

Toasty Pop is too hungry to plan. "Let's make cupcakes instead!" says Toasty.

Toasty is not a good cook. She burns the cupcakes!
"Now I'll have to buy a snack instead," Lippy says.
"Toasty, I thought we were trying to save money!"

Lippy's words give Apple Blossom an idea. "That's it!" she cries. "We can sell food at the Fall Festival and use the money to pay the power bill!" There's just one problem with Apple's plan. None of the Shopkins know how to cook.

The Shopkins practice and practice, but every meal they try to make gets ruined. They're going to need help if they want to be ready to sell treats at the festival.

Luckily, their friend Fleur Flour is a great cook.
"I'd be happy to give you all cooking lessons!"
she tells the Shopkins.

Fleur is a patient teacher. She helps Lippy make a beautiful cake.

"It's, like, so perfect. I could totally cry," says Suzie Sundae.

"You can all try a piece—but not until I take a photo!" says Lippy, whipping out her cell phone to take some snapshots.

Toasty burns her cake—again.
"This dessert is toast," she says.
"Fleur, I think I need some extra
lessons."

Fleur and Toasty practice lots of recipes together.

"The first trick of cooking is to get creative with the ingredients you have," Fleur tells Toasty.

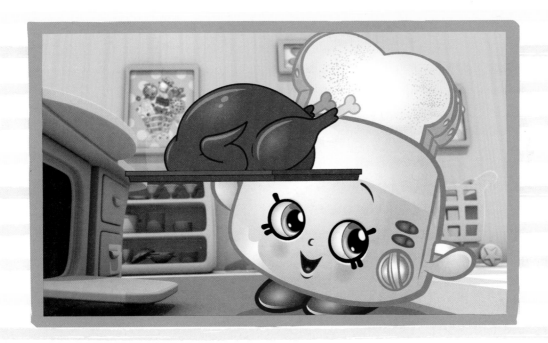

Soon, Toasty is cooking like a real chef!

Finally, after weeks of practice, it's time for the Fall Festival! It's one of the most popular events in Shopville, and the Shopkins sell lots of yummy food to their friends all day.

"We're close to our goal," says Apple Blossom. "Nothing can stop us now!"

But then dark clouds roll over Shopville. It's a storm! There's thunder, lightning, wind, and even snow—all of the Shopkins' delicious food is ruined.

The storm clears quickly, but it's too late. The Shopkins haven't made enough money to pay their bill, and there's no more food to sell.

"If the power gets turned off, I won't be able to put on my makeup!" cries Lippy.

But Toasty looks around and remembers what Fleur taught her. "I have an idea!" she says.

Toasty gets creative with one of the new ingredients she has, thanks to the storm: snow!

"Suzie, grab some flavored syrup," Toasty says. "We're making storm slushies!"

The storm slushies are a tasty hit at the festival. Every Shopkin lines up to get one!

The Shopkins pay the power bill just in time for the next episode of *The Spatula*.

"Maybe we can watch just this one . . ." says Lippy. The Shopkins settle into the couch happily.

CHECK YA LATER!